Benjamin's Portrait

Animal Portrait Gallery

In this series:
Benjamin and the Box
Benjamin's Book
Benjamin's Portrait

HAPPY CAT BOOKS

Published by Happy Cat Books Ltd,
Bradfield, Essex CO11 2UT, UK

This edition published 2004
1 3 5 7 9 10 8 6 4 2

A CIP catalogue record for this book is available from the British Library

ISBN 1 903285 93 3

Printed in China by Midas Printing International Limited

Benjamin's Portrait

ALAN BAKER

Happy Cat Books

The ears are good, but I don't like the eyes.

That's brilliant!

Ah! That's what I call a handsome beast.

Why don't I paint myself? It looks quite easy.

Paint, canvas, water, brush . . .
now it's up
to me.

First a pencil sketch.

Now to brighten it up.

I'll just get the lid off. Ah! Powder paint.

Powder's too messy . . . I'll try tubes.

Hmmmm.

Nice yellow.

Oh dear.
what a mess!

I'd better clean myself up.

Paws first.

Whoops! Help!

I *hate* being wet.

Can't do any more
till I've got myself dry.

Ahh

That's better.

Just comb my fur . . .

Now back to work.
It's a pretty good likeness already.

A little black
here and . . .

. . . it's perfect.

I'll just check the details in the mirror.

There must be an easier way to get
a perfect likeness.

Photography . . .
I shouldn't have any trouble with that.

Just hold steady and . . . ClicK!